H. D Torrey

America

Or, Visions of the Rebellion

H. D Torrey

America
Or, Visions of the Rebellion

ISBN/EAN: 9783337249465

Printed in Europe, USA, Canada, Australia, Japan

Cover: Foto ©Andreas Hilbeck / pixelio.de

More available books at **www.hansebooks.com**

America;

OR,

VISIONS OF THE REBELLION;

A POEM IN FOUR CANTOS,

BY H. D. TORREY.

Reading, Pa.:

STEAM-PRESS OF B. F. OWEN, COURT STREET.

1862.

PREFACE.

At the first writing of this poem, I had not the remotest idea of its ever appearing in public in any form; but, upon showing some parts of it to friends, in an accidental manner, their praises, and a subsequent invitation to read it publicly, induced me to give it first in a few readings, and finally in this form. Of course, in such a limited space, it will not be expected that I can give the individual exhibitions of valor and daring, or a detailed account of the incidents or battles of the war. These, with the glorious victories of our conquering army, will be traced on the historic page of our nation by master hands, and be clothed in the richest garb of poetry by the gifted of our land. Such as it is, with the purest promptings of patriotism, I offer it to the indulgence of my friends. To give it in its original form, I have prefixed it with the "Key of Explanation" used in presenting it at public readings.

H. D. TORREY.

KEY OF EXPLANATION.

BEFORE reading the poem I am about to present, I have deemed it proper to prefix a few arguments in its favor. After a severe *illness*, entirely disabling me from taking any part in putting down the great rebellion now ravaging our land, my mind being absorbed night and day with the subject, only found a partial relief in working up the figures I am about to offer. The poem has been divided in four parts, the first, third, and last, presented in the form of visions, the better to condense, and portray at a glance, the momentous interests covering so large a field. In the first part I have endeavoured to exhibit the vastness and wealth, the unparalleled beauties, and the anticipated greatness of our own loved land, and to show the dependence we should at all times acknowledge to the Almighty Being presiding over us, and how puny and weak we become when that dependence is forgotten, and we rely solely upon an arm of flesh. In concluding this brief notice to the first part, I will simply add, that it is intended to present the varied aspects of our country at the breaking out of the rebellion. The second, and principal part, treats almost exclusively of this unheard-of attempt at a dissolution of the great Union, under which we have lived so happily. Whilst it is not expected that I can embrace the individual events, which are so fast and fearfully creating the most thrilling material for coming history, although treating the subject so generally; still I have felt compelled to pause for a moment over some few of the many bloody fields and encounters in this new war of independence, as of too vital an interest, too sublime a nature, to be excluded. Some still more startling and impressive have occurred too recently to be considered here.

In the third part, which was mostly written before the reduction of Fort Sumter, I have vainly attempted to anticipate what this vast country must become, in case man can divide it into petty powers and provinces, when a continual conflict of interests, prejudices and revenges must absorb all the resources, which should be employed in developing its untold interests in every element of mental, physical and material greatness. You will see the difficulties of the task I have undertaken, and pray with me, that the fears hinted at can never be fulfilled; although, with the histories of former republics before us, and the desolation that civil war has ever entailed crowding upon our fancies, all will admit, that at least fears of such a result were more than justified.

In the fourth, and final part, I have predicted our country, rising above every obstacle at home and abroad, and taking that proud position, which, as *Americans* we love to assign her, and which she may eventually reach if her apparent destiny is fulfilled. In introducing England in the manner I have, I should say, that whether the present difficulty is temporarily adjusted or not, it is almost certain that war will eventually grow out of it, if for nothing more than to pay her for the most perfidious manner in which she has treated us, whilst administering to the wants, and encouraging the obstinacy of our enemies; thus violating all her former avowed principles and precedents. With these hasty explanations, I will present the poem to your kindest consideration.

CANTO FIRST.

In care and depression, in anguish and fear,
Dark phantoms of horror will often appear
And stalk thro' our senses, a merciless train,
'Till fancies, like visions, envelop the brain.
Again, when each nerve is aglow with delight,
Each glimpse of the future is sunny and bright,
On wings of enchantment we're wafted away,
And dream, as it were, in the glory of day.
No seal to my eyes of night's signet had come,
My muse to invoke for our country and home;
In day's brightest moments, wherever I strayed,
The fear or the hope of my song was displayed;
In 'semblance too real, again and again
It offered its pleasures, or brought me its pain.

'Mid glorious prospects, forebodings most dire,
I've seen our vast land like a pillar of fire
Attracting the gaze of a world on its crest,
Illumined with light, like a star of the west,
'Till gathering millions from every zone
Had sought its blest borders, and called them their own.
I've seen this fair fabric of Liberty rise
'Till temple and column were lost in the skies;
I've pictured it fallen—its glories unsung—
A banner of blood o'er its battlements hung;—
Have seen the last hope of its splendors expire—
Its monuments crumbled—its altars on fire,
'Till mad desolation o'er temple and dome,
Had blacken'd the fame of our Washington's home.
And thus have I dreamed of its weal and its woe—
Have seen it exultant—its greatness laid low;
And ask'd as I dream'd, if a mind could conceive—
If fancy could out of her imagery weave,

If prospered, its greatness—if fallen, the gloom

That would cover its silence, and brood o'er its tomb.

And now, had I dream'd when the future was bright—

No spell on my senses, no sleep on my sight;

Around were huge monuments, towering aloft,

With light on their summits all mellow and soft,

And emblems of valor were cut on each side,

To mark that beneath them some martyr had died;

And as I was reading each eloquent name,

That glory had given, undying, to fame,

A fairy-like creature arose on my view—

Enrobed in a vesture of red, white and blue—

Came near me and beck'ning with angelic grace,

I follow'd her steps to a monument's base,

And ent'ring an archway, she bade me ascend,

Whilst she, as a guide, my course would attend;

Oh! how shall weak language attempt to portray

The scene upon which we emerged into day!

A glass she then gave me, by which I could see
Each tint of the landscape, each isle of the sea.
A limitless country seemed drawn on my brain,
Of every land, with their mountain and plain;
The earth 'rose before me, and in its green vest
Bright rivers and fountains of silver were dressed,
And deep-tinted forests of every shade,
Flung out their cool shadows, far down o'er the glade;
Condensed in the picture, from every clime,
Was every nation and every time.
I saw in the foreground a valley of flowers—
A deep winding stream 'mid their clustering bowers,
And beautiful beings on pinions of gold,
Were lifting its waters so limpid and cold,
And soaring away in their vestments of white,
'Till lost in the glow of etherial light,
I follow'd their flight, till there flashed on my eye
A dazzling city above in the sky.

Oh, beautiful vision ! above and below,

The earth and the heavens were all in a glow—

Down, down from the city, a wonderful gleam

Shot out, to illumine the valley and stream ;

There hamlet and cottage—familiar and strange—

Peer'd up from some hillside or wild mountain range,

And gorgeous palaces, churches and towers,

Arose from their settings of emerald bowers ;

And then, through the lenses all brilliant and bright,

I saw my own country spread out in the light,

And rays from the city I still saw above,

Were flooding its realms in a halo of love.

I asked the fair goddess who stood by my side—

Her title and emblems I now had discried—

To solve the strange myst'ry her vision revealed,

And showing some mottoes engraved on her shield,

She bade me read o'er them ; and written in light,

Independence I saw, and *Religion* and *Right*,

Constitution and *Law*, *Education* and more
I turned to my eye and read o'er and o'er.
"These, these are all emblems." she said, "of each beam
That falls from above in that heavenly stream;
And I am a messenger thence, to preside
O'er this beautiful land that spreads far and wide.
So long as you turn to the city you see
For light and support. so long you are free;
But shut off the fountain—forget whence it comes—
And darkness will hang o'er your desolate homes."
Then, asking her glass in the blandest of tone,
The Goddess of Liberty left me alone;
Entreating me still, as she flitted from sight,
To stand by those mottoes—look upward for light;
Assuring me too, if true I'd remain,
The power of those lenses my eye would retain;
She plumed her bright pinions and vanished in flight,
But left on my vision the marvelous sight.

I saw from that column that Freedom had reared,
To note the proud death of its children revered,
What still would inspire an American heart,
And make the warm life-blood of Liberty start;
Around, in the glorious sunlight of day,
My own and the homes of my forefathers lay.
Arcadian beauties to tameness would fade,
Compared with the picture by fancy portrayed—
The meadow and valley, and forest and hill—
The leaping cascade, with the river and rill.
The deep-mirrored lakes, where a thousand white sail
Flew merrily on with their wings to the gale,
Spread out o'er the scene with the sky in their breast,
Like jewels of light on the brow of the west,
Where huge floating palaces steamed thro' the tide,
With deep-burthened barges, that clung to their side,
O'erladen with traffic, and travel, and trade,
In wondrous bounty of plenty displayed.

A million of furnaces, forges and mills,
Their blue smoke sent upward to soften the hills.
Along by the stream on the steep mountain side,
The fast running wheel had industry supplied;
From broad smiling pastures, the gentle kine lowed—
From barn-yard and stable, brave chanticleer crowed,
And timed-eyed sheep in white armies were seen
To feed or repose in the beautiful green.
Stout husbandmen toil or rest at the door,
Contented and happy that labor is o'er;
No shade on their features of sorrow can rest—
Their lot has been cast in the land of the blest.
Along the broad turn-pike we hear the glad song,
As wag'ner and driver are urging along
The huge muscled team, with its ponderous cart,
As travel or produce would come and depart.
From mowers and reapers at work in the vale,
The shout of thanksgiving mounts up on the gale;

Where'er the eye wanders, where'er we give ear,

There is something to charm us and something to cheer.

Blithe martins seem warbling their musical roles,

From snug little cots on the tops of their poles,

And every ut'rance seems vocal with praise,

From the bay of the dog to the robin's soft lays.

There's music in nature, around and above,

O'er mountain and valley, through forest and grove ;

'Tis heard in the sigh of the gentle cascade,

The winds sweep its numbers o'er river and glade ;

The wild mountain stream as it murmers along

Flings up from its windings the rapture of song ;

Each log thrown athwart it, each rock it winds by,

Lifts up from its bosom a chaunt to the sky.

'Mid tropical verdure, from prairies and trees,

The songs, as of nature inspired, never cease ;

Its whispering trill, or its anthem most grand,

Yield musical praise for our own blessed land.

"Oh! where," I exclaimed, "where else on the earth
Except in this Éden, could Freedom find birth."
Oh, favored of nature—more favored of heaven—
The lovliest country to man ever given—
Oh! where, gracious Lord do such blessings combine
To stamp on earth's kingdoms, Thy presence divine!
There, sev'ring the distance, tho' dimly displayed,
Strange pathways of iron, unending, are laid,
And hither and thither, like a comet at play,
Some monster in harness leaps forth on its way;
Now spanning some stream on the ponderous bridge,
Now darting like light 'long the rock-crested ridge—
A scream and a puff and it springs from our sight,
Like a meteor coursing the heavens at night,
Terrific, o'erwhelming, yet held by some plan,
To pause or advance at the bidding of man;
Communities follow its lightning-like trail,
And cleave like an arrow its firm-belted rail.

Wherever we turn there is something to charm,
And keep the heart's blood of the patriot warm;
There, nestled in comfort, some cottage is seen—
A dot of pure white on its back-ground of green;
The old country school-house, with children at play,
Seems e'en where we gathered in youth's sunny day.
By rivers wide-bosomed, vast cities arise,
With steeple and dome looming up to the skies;
Intelligence, industry, science and art
Combine in their borders vast truths to impart;
Amusement and mirth, and religion and song,
Each thrill in their turn to enrapture the throng;
There commerce relieved has set down her rich store,
Or spreads her wide wings as she journeys for more;
Refinement and riches, and luxury come
To find in these marts their appropriate home;
The murmur of business, the bustle of trade,
The streets of the city have eloquent made;

There, wonderful presses by magic are taught
To burthen the world with their treasures of thought :
Whilst invention and genius, with labor combine
To cheer and reward us—enlarge and refine ;
The vot'ries of pleasure, of letters and law,
'Round centres of learning and eloquence draw
The plaudits of millions from village and town,
Who glory and pride in their country's renown;
Thus, varied and beautiful, drawn on the eye,
Do Freedom's most glorious emoluments lie.
I heard a great wail of unutterable woe,
And the monument reeled on its granite below.
I left its proud top, as I saw everywhere
Thick mists of foreboding obscuring the air,
And thought of the goddess, her mottoes and shield—
Looked up for the light, which was partly concealed ;
And felt, that though beauteous the mottoes might be,
'Twas only by light their designs we could see.

CANTO SECOND.

When treason's black hand was first dastardly thrust
To pluck the bright meeds o'er our forefather's dust,
'Twas urged that one-half of the North would arise
To help pull the stars from that flag in the skies,
And cringing and crawling from some noisome hole,
With blood on their skirts and a blot on their soul,
Vile creatures did come, with their heart in their hand,
Determined to sever this glorious land ;
And recreant sons of brave patriot sires,
Were sworn to extinguish our national fires,
And rear o'er their ashes a throne in their stead,
Where tyrants could gloat o'er the once-honored dead;
But masses of men in our fair northern clime
Shrank back with dismay at so fearful a crime,

And swore in their hearts, without party or name,   .
To stand by those altars or die in their shame;
And up from each house-top, there leaped in surprise
A legion of banners to gladden the skies.
From farm-house and fact'ry, from valley and glen,
Was heard the fierce tramping of brave-hearted men;
And flashing new fire in the hearts of the brave,
Her cannon's loud thunder boomed over the wave,
The glory of Sumter rose far o'er its flame,
Embalming its heroes forever in fame.
And forth from its capture, its breaches and blood,
A pæan more potent was borne o'er the flood,
Than ever war's clarion wakened before,
To thrill the vast hosts of its legions of yore;
And History's pages will show doubly bright,
The name of her ANDERSON written in light—
That brave band of warriors that walled him around,
Shall live in the depths of affection profound,

And mothers point out to the child at their knee,
That spot where their fathers had struck for the free.
Oh! there was a scene 'mid those hot, smoking walls,
The bursting of shells and the battering balls,
As furious flames leaped forth through the fort,
And stifled the air in their hidious sport.
To which the redeem'd—even God in delight,
Could bend as befitting emaculate sight,
When ANDERSON clustered his men in despair,
And gave his great soul to his Maker in prayer!
Methinks some bright angel hung low on his wing,
Full, answering responses of comfort to bring,
And even the heavens had borrowed a ray,
Whilst he and his warriors had gathered to pray.
If ever the human can borrow divine,
And mortal o'erreach immortality's line,
'Tis when the great chieftain, the gen'ral, unseals
His heart-breaking faith in such prayerful appeals.

The weight of such prayers, in their power to save,
Should rescue a nation from anarchy's grave.
But now, the black coils of disunion entwined
Its loathsome embraces 'round body and mind,
And struck in the dark by its venemous tooth,
Its victims were found in the temples of truth;
In court and in senate, in councils of might,
It drew its dark length like a shadow of night,
And charmed by the song of its poisonous breath—
No station was safe from this demon of death;
It breathed on the oath of allegiance, and lo!
From that sacred relic its poison would flow;
It wound through the army and places of state,
And buried its fangs in the gifted and great;
And under the semblance of friendship and love.
It came with the seeming and song of the dove,
And Judas-like, kissing its master to-day,
To-morrow, like Judas, went forth to betray.

*   *   *   *   *

Already the carcass is severed in twain,

And every contortion is wreathing in pain ;

The heel of stern Justice is poising to-day

Its weight on the head of the reptile to lay.

And soon the mad fiat of wrath shall go forth,

To banish this fiend from the places of earth ;

Oh ! God speed the moment, when back it must go

To crawl with its kindred in regions below.

'Tis true the dark waves of secession rolled high—

A moment obscuring the smiles of the sky—

But marks of its ruin, self-punishing lay

O'er realms of its own, that had welcomed its sway ;

For when it had deluged the land where it 'woke,

And on its own bosom received the foul stroke,

The iron-like Keystone her barriers preferred,

And o'er her broad bulwarks no tempest was heard,

And Bay-State and Empire, the Buckeye and all,

With fair little Rhody, so great (yet so small),
Sent forth from their children the stoutest and best,
To keep the dark waves from their forefathers' rest;
"Thus far shalt thou go," we have said to their bands,
And hemmed in with ruin their desolate lands;
For when our brave LINCOLN his summons sent forth,
It seemed that its echoes had startled the earth;
From glorious Maine and her forests untold,
To proud California's rich valleys of gold;
Across from the east to the far, mighty west,
There came a response, as from Liberty's breast,
And sons of the North are now seen ev'rywhere,
With weapons and banners borne forth on the air;
And 'round that proud ensign emblazoned by time,
Are gathering patriots from every clime;
From snows of the Alps and the Arctic combine
Brave warriors with those of the fabulous Rhine;
The German and Cossack, Italian and Hun.

Now find all their countries united in one ;
One country, one flag, and one cause they espouse,
And offer their blood and their lives, with their vows.
The son of fair Erin looks off o'er the sea,
And sighs, as he strikes with the sons of the free.
Let brightest of meeds, and the dearest of rights,
Descend on the hero who fearlessly fights
For what he adopted, on turning his eyes
From scenes of his birth to American skies ;
We hail him as brother, and clasping the hand,
Would make him at home in our own native land ;
And gathering now with our panoplied throng,
Such heroes as these, with our own, march along,
And stout must the arm be and mighty the hand,
To measure its strength with this conquering band ;
They strike not for plunder, they fight not for place ;
The flag that they love has been trailed in disgrace,
And impious feet on that banner have trod,

They honored and worshiped as next to their God.

The brothers they loved, born of one common sire,

Against that kind parent have dared to conspire,

And monsters, inhuman, are seeking his life,

And clutch at his throat with the blood-recking knife.

They shatter the home of their childhood and birth,

And o'er their foul carnage hold merciless mirth.

Our time-honored charter of rights they ignore,

And swear its firm compacts shall bind them no more,

Or hang, like a felon, who still would be true

And stand by those record our ancestors drew.

For this, and for more, do our legions advance

To cross with these boasters the sabre and lance,

And God help the right, when we meet face to face,

To wipe out the stain of their damning disgrace.

Already a hundred fierce conflicts have told,

No star can be torn from that ensign of old,

And up from Fort Donelson frowning on high,

With barbette and bastion drawn out on the sky,
There leaps a wild shout from our hosts gathered there,
To startle with glory the sulphurous air;
Up, up to the ramparts, 'mid bat'ry and ball,
Brave Smith and his men cut their way to the wall,
And cutlass and sabre, and bayonet tell
Where thousands of traitors ingloriously fell,
Whilst aghast at our daring, the fratricides cower
And shrink from the stroke of infuriate power.
Indiana and Iowa, sisters in might,
Together have battled and conquered for right,
And on o'er dead comrades and brothers fresh slain,
All mangled, and mingled in heaps on the plain—
On, on o'er companion and traitor the same,
Through bristling bayonets, bullets and flame;
O'er life-lamps expiring, and hopes that burn low,
The brave Illinoisons exultingly go—
No force can repulse them, no power can withstand

Their charge on the foe, as they strike hand to hand.
Ohio's and Michigan's bravest are there—
The flags of secession from Donelson tear ;
Like waves of the ocean on some rocky shore,
The sons of the West in their majesty pour,
And melting before them, proud hosts turn away
And leave the brave Northmen the lords of the day.
And now, as the lightnings obedient flash,
Our infantry's charges, our cavalry's dash,
And liberty's legions triumphantly leap
To banish their foes from the perilous deep,
A monster, submerged to the lip in the flood,
In iron sails forth on her mission of blood ;
How god-like she moves in impervious mail,
Disgorging her shot 'mid the quivering sail.
And how, for a moment, wide echoes resound,
As answering responses are op'ning around,
And how our brave seamen insensibly quail

As shot strike those sheathings, and scatter like hail
From roofs struck in summer by some passing shower,
And glance unaccompanied by purpose or power!
Not valor, nor daring, with fate may contend,
And God only knows how the contest may end.
O'er hearts never flinching, fall shivering spars,
And ruin leaps mad 'neath the fluttering stars,
Whilst swift, massive missiles are mowing our decks,
Resolving our Navy to figureless wrecks!
But see! In the distance, half sunk in the foam,
Some object is seen through the waters to roam;
It nears, and a flame is belched forth from its tow'r—
Omnipotence shines in its prestige and power—
And on comes the *Monitor* startling the sight—
Combatting, like David, this giant of might;
Like two maddened bison, death-locked on the plain,
They grapple, and goring, shrink back on the main
To gather new muscle the charge to decide,

And settle their fate on the unconcerned tide.

Ah! see how the Merimac shirks the embrace,

And hies from the combat in wounded disgrace.

Brave WORDEN has conquered, and shouts leap on high

To hallow the air of the far bending sky!

And long as a mast, or a mizzen, shall bear

A sail or a flag to the freshening air,

Commander and maker of that little craft

In plaudits, immortal, the future shall waft.

At Roanoke, Winchester, Pea-Ridge and Fort Brown

The deeds of our soldiers were bathed in renown!

See glorious SIEGEL, with sabre in hand.

Encountering single that murderous band.

Each circuit that follows his powerful blow

Sends Southern or Savage imploring below.

How fair over Winchester's carnage awoke—

O'er its valor and brav'ry—its thunder and smoke—

A fame, our loved Keystone shall clasp to her breast,

Whilst she 'mid the states is still binding the rest!

Her sons, as they fell in their sanctified gore,

Adorned the fair name of their state evermore,

And the Eighty-Fourth's slaughter and deeds will be

sung

While Liberty's accents can startle the young.

The lion-like SHIELDS, with his great Irish heart,

No more from the memory of freemen can part,

And long as the harp or the shamrock retain,

A tone for the heart or a thought for the brain,

American patriots will turn with a smile

To greet the brave sons of the Emerald Isle,

As on with our ranks, like the unsubdued sea,

They dash in the strength of the mighty and free,

'Till every traitor on every field,

To valorous freemen their banners must yield.

Here linger with me ye bravest of brave—

A moment to sigh o'er the Cumberland's grave—

In sadness turn with me, ye stoutest of heart,
And see that good ship on her mission depart!
Oh! well may the god of the watery deep,
As such martyrs sink to his chambers to sleep,
Exultingly startle his billowy sky
With shouts o'er the heroes who come there to die!
Oh! where on the blood-written page of the past—
'Mid carnage, or battle, or thunder, or blast—
Where! where, since a rudder has guided a keel,
And decks have been crimsoned by bullet and steel,
Oh! where went there down in the pitiless wave,
A cargo so precious to one common grave!
Ye nations, whose glory is writ on the sea,
Draw nigh for a moment with Freedom and me,
And hear that brave crew, as they sink in their gloom,
A requiem chaunt o'er their own yawning tomb—
A volley discharge o'er their own briny bier,
As they and their ship, from that flag disappear;

They shrink not, they quail not, but martyr-like, sip
The billow and blood, on their fast sinking ship.
Oh! long will it be ere the future can tell
Where men fought so bravely, or died half so well.
Our Navy, our Army, our Nation will keep
Like jewels the mem'ries of those in the deep;
A tear wrung from pity, yet hallowed with pride,
We drop o'er our brothers asleep 'neath the tide,
And turn with emotion we cannot conceal,
Again to new objects, our muse would reveal.

    *   *   *   *   *

A new race of chieftains now tread our broad land,
And time never marshalled a mightier band,
Our old giant SCOTT, although oldest and best,
The bravest and truest, above all the rest,
Now sees the bright names of a legion appear
His sunset of life and its glory to cheer;
May God spare him longer, to country and kind,

And leave when he goes his bright mantle behind ;
And now may M'CLELLAN, enveloped in might,
With truth for his armor, and girded with right,.
Invoke the pure light from above on his cause.
And conquer or die for our union and laws.
May SIEGEL and CURTIS, and BUEL and GRANT,
Their flags o'er the ramparts of treachery plant,
May HALLECK and SHERMAN, DUPONT and brave
    POPE
Inspire their brave men with the conqueror's hope ;
May BURNSIDE and GOLDSBOROUGH glory combine,
Their brows with the palm and the cypress to twine,
And BUTLER and GEARY, and FOOT and the rest
Still keep their great hearts throbbing high in each
    breast ;
May CORCORAN feel in the cell of the slave
The love he inspires in the hearts of the brave ;
Our brothers o'erpowered by a vile southern horde,

Gaze back with new hope where their names are ador'd.

May every private and every man—

The wounded and sick, and the weak of our clan,

Exist while our future has power to inspire—

Our nation the acts of its brave can admire.

A long list of chieftains in pride I could bring,

And Fame o'er each title her garlands would fling,

But acts of the living I'll not recount here,

The future will tell how their names must appear;

So let them be true to each hope and each trust,

In faith that their cause and that future is just;

And freemen unborn yet will chaunt their brave deeds,

And gaze with delight on their glorious meeds;

But let the bright laurels unfadingly twine

And blossom in love o'er the new martyr's shrine;

Can memories of LYON and ELLSWORTH expire,

And die with the death of the brief battle fire?

Shall blood have no voices where BAKER was slain,

To thrill in the future his glory again?
Shall GREBLE and WARD with their deeds pass away,
And rouse not our sons in the far coming day?
So long as the flag of Columbia waves
A fold o'er the sod of their eloquent graves,
Or muscle, or sinew, or blood shall remain
In country or purpose akin to the slain,
So long, like sweet incense, their names shall arise
Exultingly up to their home in the skies;
Oh! let the last gasp, and the last parting sigh
Be yielded to such, if our nation must die;
Their names on our lips and their worth in our heart,
Thus true to the past let our spirits depart.
Then, sunk in the gloom of our gory decay—
The flag from our ramparts in shame torn away,
When voices leap forth from the tombs of the past,
To pour their reproach on the requiem blast,
Oh! then may all Europe come forth o'er the waves,

To build up their thrones o'er republican graves;
But while there's a shred of our banner on high—
A stripe or a star to illumine the sky—
A throb of that glory that hallowed the past,
And carried our fathers through tempest and blast,
To tingle the veins of their children again,
Oh! let their proud legions come not o'er the main;
The world, though encased in an armor of might,
Must shrink from the blows of invincible right;
We say to earth's despots and tyrants, beware!
A storm o'er your thrones is now stirring the air,
And throes of an earthquake seem heaving below,
Its elements rife with destruction and woe.
But hark! a new shout comes from valley and glen,
And crowding the highways are hurrying men;
The young and the stalwart, the aged and all
Are pouring from palace, from cottage and hall;
Some fresh inspiration has fired every heart,

And bade the old leven of Liberty start.

Like vast living tides, with their weapons in hand,

A million of freemen are flooding the land,

And women, brave women, American wives,

Who shrink not in danger to peril their lives,

Are urging their husbands, their brothers and sons,

To leave them the care of the dear little ones,

And help through the danger, the conflict and all,

To burnish the rifle or model the ball,

To comfort the able, the daring and brave,

Or tend the dead hero in peace to his grave;

Oh woman! dear woman! in trial and death,

Through every change from our earliest breath,

The ministering angel thou ever hast ever been—

A light to the path of poor care-burthened men.

     *   *   *   *   *

What stern resolution—what purpose has come

To call forth these warriors from hamlet and home;

They come not forth now, as with brother to war—
To quiet the broil of a family jar,
Some direful revenge, like a venomous sore
Seems bleeding afresh, that was given of yore;
Ah, see! the invader on Freedom's fair land,
Has come from afar to this traitorous band;
Brave England forgets, as she thinks our hands tied,
For what we have battled—for what we have died—
The lessons we taught her, when we were but young,
And first to the tempest our frail banner flung—
Forgets how we scattered her armies before,
And drove them in shame from our blood-hallowed
        shore,
How the Eagle went up, as the Lion went down,
To crouch in the blood by his profligate crown.
She lays her red hand on that page of the past,
Which still o'er her wrecks and her ruin shall last
To tell of the shock that Old Ironsides gave

A navy they boasted as lord of the wave;

The cross and the Lion was struck oft and oft,

As our bunting of starlight flew proudly aloft;

She closes her eyes to those blood-deluged scenes,

From Lexington reaching to proud New Orleans,

And fancies the links in that magical chain

Encircl'ing the Union from Texas to Maine,

Disjointed and riven; and hails with delight

The blood on each coupling once burnished and bright.

Oh shame, selfish England! to cower to-day,

And barter your glory because it will pay.

For years you have coin'd from your ponderous mouth,

Harsh words and abuse, for the misguided South;

But whilst you were cous'ning and courting our blacks,

It seems have been braiding new thongs for their backs.

  *   *   *   *   *

United, they feared us—divided, they'd come

To fatten their cubs where our young eaglets roam;

Let them take poor old Mason—the wretched Slidell,
And toast them, and feast them, and flatter them well,
The vipers they'd warm from a traitorous death,
Have cursed and have stung them at every breath,
But let them not think, that by fear or by threats,
We yielded the care of their troublesome pets ;
Stern justice, though slow, is e'er following crime—
Their base-hearted act, is but biding its time,
For England, mad England ! a spark still endures,
And when our sharp swords shall leap forth to meet
      yours,
Its flames shall flash upward, a world to inspire
And thrill, at the vastness of liberty's fire ;
And when you have dared the avenger, to wreak
The vengeance that you have so long shown the
      weak,
Farewell to thy prestige o'er land and o'er sea,
For God will forsake both the banner and thee,

And right, and religion, humanity too,
Will side with our eagle 'gainst treason and you.

    *   *   *   *   *

Again the fierce jargon of battle swells forth
And draws in its vortex the nations of earth,
Vast kingdoms, and empires, are pouring their blood
To deepen the hue of the far-swelling flood ;
All Europe inhaling the breath from afar,
Has welcomed the dawn of Christianity's war,
And now as her thrones and sceptres give way,
I see a new dawning of liberty's day—
The Emerald Island now leaps from the sea,
Her harps all attuned to the songs of the free
Her brave-hearted sons are beginning to feel
Their necks working clear from the Briton's hard heel,
As up from the green of their own native sod,
They stand forth erect in the image of God.
But whilst there was danger or doubt in the sky,

And nothing but chaos to sadden the eye,

My fancy, disheartened, had seen in its gloom

The death of our country, and stood by its tomb.

In visions, I saw the republics of old

Go out with their treasures of glory untold ;

The bandit I saw in their once pop'lous street,

Glide noiselessly by on his treacherous feet,

Or steal to some covert, with pistol and knife—

No safety to virtue, no warrant of life,

And thought what our own blessed country would be,

If men could dismember this home of the free,

And sorely depressed at each fanciful gleam,

Though sleepless as day, yet again I would dream.

CANTO THIRD.

I saw as I dreamed, what had seemed to me,
A white crested ship on a silvery sea—
The sea wore a sheen as of silvery hue,
And yet it was radiant with crimson and blue,
And meteors shot forth o'er its waters so bright—
Enshrouding that bark in their phosphorent light,
'Till glowing like gold, on the billows afar
It showed on each mast-head a beautiful star;
And up from the ocean, at intervals rise
Huge beacon-towers, rearing their lamps to the skies;
And each threw a ray as of dazzling glare,
Diverging its light on the ship that was there.
How proud they all look, and numbering them o'er
I find, in delight, they count thirty-four.

How noble, how graceful that vessel rode there,
Her delicate lines cutting sharp on the air—
And now I could see as she danced in her pride,
" *The Union*," in letters of gold, on her side.
" Oh, beautiful model !" I cried as she flew,
An arrow of light, through the ocean's deep blue
Beyond, and around, on the neighboring strand,
Arose in prospective, proud nations and lands,
Where signals and rockets were streaming above,
To welcome this craft on her mission of love ;
And millions of voices rang out on the sky,
To startle the stillness entrancing the eye ;
Oh, vision resplendent ! I now could discern
The crew and the rigging from bow-sprit to stern—
Each one I beheld had a badge with his name,
That beamed from his breast-plate in letters of flame ;
I saw a bright banner flung out overhead,
With field of pure azure and stripes of deep red ;

And soon, a bright star from each beacon-light came

To shed on its flaunting their own lambent flame ;

An eagle came down from its heavenward flight,

And perched on that pennant refulgent with light.

There stood the great helmsman, and watching his

      eye,

I saw that he gazed far above on the sky

To luminous fountains, that sent a warm flood

Of light on the deck, where the proud hero stood—

'Twas WASHINGTON held the stout helm as I gazed,

For written in glory his title was blazed ;

And FRANKLIN and ADAMS, and JACKSON and CLAY,

And others as true and stout-hearted as they,

Were sharing the cares and the joys of the trip—

Their treasures and jewels all locked in that ship ;

And when from the helm the great pilot withdrew,

Each one took his turn to help steer the ship through ;

I saw, whilst careening, some deep cruel scar—

Some patch in her rigging, some break in a spar—
By red in each seam, as she shot o'er the flood,
I saw that her planks were cemented in blood,
Which told of fierce battles, and shocks she had passed,
Though worthy and staunch, she had proven at last;
And onward she flew in her beauty and might—
The fear of the guilty, the hope of the right.
I gazed as entranced on this wonderful scene,
More startling and brilliant than ever was seen,
When off in the distance, a speck I espied
Borne nearer and nearer along o'er the tide,
'Till larger and darker exposed to the sight,
Each throb of my nature was stifled with fright;—
The speck proved a monster whose hideous form,
Had beaten those waves to a pitiless storm—
Like legions of darkness huge clouds clove the sky,
And from their deep shadows the tempest rushed by;
I turn to the waters—Oh God what a sight!—

That late tranquil surface is lashed into fright,
And demon-like spectres, seem treading the waves,
Like fiends coming forth from their billowy graves,
And soon the bright towers go down in their gloom,
To crumble away in their fathomless tomb,
While phantoms of phrenzy seem crowding the air,
As matter would back to its chaos repair;
I saw this proud ship with the Union in view,
The last hope of Freedom plunge down with her crew,
And heard a vast cry as of liberty dead,
Afar on the wings of the hurricane spread.

     *   *   *   *   *

In sadness and sorrow I turned from the scene,
And gazed on the land in its limitless green;
But oh! as I looked, how the blood in each vein
Seemed curdled, or seeking its fountain again;
'Twixt me and the blue of the heavens afar,
Hang colums of smoke o'er the clangor of war,

Whilst thousands of brothers are grappling there,

With victory's shoutings, or vanquished despair.

Exultant, triumphant, up, up to the sky,

Huzzas from the host of the conquering fly,

And on o'er the roar of the carnage again

I catch the death moaning—the shrieking of pain ;

Stout hearts and huge statures are clutching to-day,

To conquer or die in the bloody affray.

I see that proud emblem, once hallowed with light—

Our fathers had borne over conflict and fight—

A mongrel one near it, with half of its blue,

And half of its stars, and the stripes formed anew ;

And curses are raised o'er the rents and the scars,

That traitors have made in that banner of stars ;

They flutter unequal, advance and retire—

Forever the old one seems fluttering higher—

'Till arms that uplift them are cloven in twain,

And standard and bearer go down with the slain.

Oh, God! must that flag all undimmed as of yore
Ne'er grace undivided Columbia more?

  *   *   *   *   *

The sons of those fathers, who once side by side,
For Freedom and Union had battled and died,
Now glare on each other all clotted with gore,
And curse what was kindred and country before.
The eagle swoops not from his home in the sky,
But shrinks like a vulture away from the eye;
No longer the pride of the measureless air,
His scream is the cravens—his shriek is despair;
A monster seems shrouding the sky with its wings,
And dire desolation her dark shadow flings,
To blot as it were with a vision of woe,
The hope-tints of Freedom once proudly aglow.

  *   *   *   *   *

Thou country of Washington, Jackson and Clay,
Must thy greatness cease, and their fame pass away?

And from that bright record of patriots and men,
Can they not be uttered in glory again ?
My Country! Columbia! in visions of thee,
Through fate's darkened mirror, thy future I see ;
O'er bright smiling regions run rivers of gore,
Where plentiful harvests were rip'ning before ;
The plough and the anvil, the loom and the spade,
Unused and forgotten, are carelessly laid
To rust in the furrow, or rot in the mill,
While clamor of workshops and forges, is still.
The axe of the woodsman, sounds not on the air,
The sword and the rifle, and death have been there.
Plantation, and meadow, wood, garden, and glen,
Re-echo no more the glad voices of men ;
The inn is deserted, and silence has spread
A pall of dismay o'er the homes of the dead.
About the red fire of the furnace's glare,
With sinews of iron, no groups gather there

Expectant with hope, that when homeward they turn
To carry the dear ones the mite they may earn,
Contentment and comfort, religion, will come
To thrill ev'ry heart 'round the altar and home;
That fire has gone out, and the home is laid low,
And houseless, and foodless, the wanderers go;
The quick pulse of commerce is spent on the sea—
The flag that droops o'er it no longer is free;
The white-winged vessels no longer explore
The climate and country of every shore,
Returning deep-laden with treasures and gold,
In marvelous value of riches untold;
But torn sails above them hang idly at play,
O'er stout oaken hulls that are seeking decay,
The rigging, in shreds, drops unused from the mast
That once threw its spars to the storm and the blast;
Rank grass is o'ergrowing the wharf and the quay,
And mildew o'erspreading our marts by the sea.

No longer our Navy is honored afar
And hailed as the advent of Liberty's star;
Proud nations now pass it in withering scorn,
And sneer at our banner all bloody and torn.

    *   *   *   *   *

I see, as the car of War's Juggernaut rolls,
The sacrifice made in the writhing of souls;
The temple up-reared to the worship of God,
The foot of the vandal and robber has trod.
That shrine of affection, the old burial ground,
The touch of pollution has shamelessly found.
And ivy and willow—the rose in its bloom—
Are scattered and torn from the family tomb;
The shafts of pure marble, that memory reared,
With couplets of sorrow, have all disappeared,
And steeds of grim warriors are tramping to-day,
O'er graves, where the bones of our loved ones lay.
The school-house all vacant, its shutters unhung,

Is vocal no more with the shouts of the young,
But sentries are pacing o'er gravel and grass,
Where childhood was wont in its rompings to pass,
The marts of the merchant, the college and hall,
Now sleap 'neath the night of a desolate pall.

CANTO FOURTH.

AGAIN the dark waves have careered on their way,
Revealing in wonder a glorious day;
Baptised like their fathers in rivers of blood,
The giants of Freedom come forth from the flood,
Renewed in devotion by bullets and steel,
And 'round the fair shrines of Columbia kneel.
The Dahlgreen and Parott are burnished no more,
To peal through the valley their death-dealing roar,
And cutlass and sabre, unused by brave men,
Leap back well-appeased to their scabbards again.
A vision of peace and of plenty once more
Has dawned o'er the ocean, and over the shore,
And brighter than ever across our fair sky,
The rainbow of promise and hope I descry.

The watch-fires of Freedom from every hill
Are burning more brilliant and beautiful still,
And now our great nation is what it professed,
The hope of the fallen, the weak and oppressed.
Now farther and wider o'er every sea,
Shall float that dear emblem, the Flag of the Free;
From far Oregon, on whose pebbly shore
The depths of Pacific its thunderings pour,
And o'er its vast waters to numberless isles
That slumber in odors 'neath tropical smiles,
It floats o'er a Navy that none dare despise,
And flashes its power wherever it flies.
From graves of our kindred, this blood-hallowed earth,
Made sacred to man by its Washington's birth,
From hearts that throb on it, and hopes it inspires,
Its emblems of grandeur—its Liberty's fires;
From treason subdued and its hirelings acurst,
Its army o'erpowered and its minions dispersed—

From greatness and glory, as even its shame,

Our nation is carving a mightier name;—

A name that shall linger in every clime,

More brilliant and fair to the fullness of time,

And up from this soil where our fathers are lain—

Their sons poured fresh blood for its safety again—

Far up to the vault of the azure above—

In power, and plenitude, honor and love,

A monument rises, with column so high

That bondsmen can see as they turn the glad eye

The love and affection, its grandeur enshroud—

The light on its summit above the dark cloud,

'Tis liberty's shaft, and its lantern above

Is flashing abroad its effulgence of love ;—

It streams o'er the ocean a pathway of light,

And glares in the dungeons of anarchy's night,

Illumines the cells of the crushed and oppressed,

And turns their glad eyes to the land of the west ;

And titles, and sceptres, and thrones, shall give way,
And melt in the glow of regenerate day ;
And God shall bend down from His glory afar,
To bring us safe forth from this fratricide war,
Whilst back from new altars, fresh incense shall rise,
Responsive with praise, to the radiant skies—
And here 'mid our mountains, and valleys so green,
Glad pilgrims from earth's farthest bounds shall
      convene,
To wait with our children, the trump's final blast
To summon us all with its fiat at last.
Oh, land of Columbia ! thou home of the free
Such, such thy vast future is pictured to me.
Thus far, the Great Spirit, with pillar of flame,
Has guarded our trials, our triumphs and fame ;—
He stood by the Pilgrims on Plymoth's lone rock—
Our patriot sires in the battle's fierce shock—
In weal and in woe, in its peace and its wars

His smile ever following the eagle and stars,
Has hovered, dispelling all doubting and fear
From scenes of His choice, and His temples reared here.
Oh ! still may we turn our glad eyes for the light
That fell from the city so holy and bright—
The deeds of our future grow bright in the same,
And catch on their records its luminous flame;
May He who has guided our dest'nies before,
Still lead and direct us in right evermore ;
And still may He bend in His goodness and might,
To hallow the land He has flooded with light.

THE END.